NOTHING KILLS THE SUN

ZANE PALMER

Zane Palmer

Zane Palmer

Nothing Kills the Sun

Zane Palmer

Zane Palmer

ACTS

Zane Palmer

Zane Palmer

THE *INTRO*

By the year 2155 Earth could no longer sustain the growing human population. Mankind had prospered after surviving near extinction resulting in a civilization-wide baby boom. The leaders of Earth put aside their differences and came together to form Earth United.

In 2158, Earth United's first summit discussed the environmental risks of population growth. Their first order was to declare a thirty-three-year ban on childbirth.

Their second order declared that mankind must begin its expansion into space. The council of Earth United concluded their summit with their third order. Additional continents would be constructed over the oceans. These massive man made landforms would stand on pillars spread out around the world. The pillars were designed to shift with the tectonic plates of the planet below.

The first constructed continent Atlanticanera took two generations across seventy-five years to complete. The landmass spanned the North Atlantic Ocean connecting four continents with its borders. By the year 2250 three other continents were under development. In the beginning, only the wealthiest could afford to live in the new lands.

The first order of Earth United was never lifted for those who could not or chose not to leave the natural surface. The Council determined that children raised on the surface would not be prosperous. Those caught during pregnancy or with a child were arrested. We were looked down upon as nothing.

My life is living proof that they're wrong.

My name is Hammers Nole, and I was born illegally in 2391 in the Kansas Wastelands of North America. My parents broke a two-hundred-and-fifty-year-old law to give me life. When I was still a child men from the EU police force known as Sentries found our small nomadic community. I don't recall much about my mother, but the older I get the more I see her in my reflection.

My father's lifeless face after the Sentries found us has haunted me ever since.

The children from our community became the property of the EU. I was selected along with another boy to be recruited into the Sentries. I swore an oath to serve the ones who uprooted my life and saw me as nothing.

THE *MISSION*

Yesterday, I was pulled from my unit and placed on a transport shuttle with four other Sentries. The flying craft soared through the clouds toward Higher-Asiaopia, the tallest continent. It was a sight so beautiful it felt like we were ascending into the heavens. The three men in the shuttle bickered over who got the window seat, a luxury in our cramped quarters. I offered the other woman next to me a chance to lean over for a better view, but she declined.

After our ship landed we were greeted by a fellow Sentry who introduced himself as Adrian.

He briefed us on our security detail and then escorted us off the landing pad and into the building below. The architecture was unlike anything I'd seen before, both inside and out. The corridors were bathed in light as Adrian guided us to a large chamber.

Inside the air buzzed with anticipation. Men and women in suits mingled with those in lab coats, but we were the only Sentries, which felt off to me.

We gave Adrian our thanks as he showed us our seats. Once we were situated he dismissed himself to stand guard outside. At each station, thick envelopes of paperwork awaited us.

We circled the center of the room, where A pair of lab coats had already set up. Their equipment projected a 360-degree image of an Earth that felt foreign to me.

"As you can see from these satellite images," the lead astrophysicist said. His lanky arm stretched out toward a holographic globe. Despite the view, my eyes kept pulling away to the tuffs of dark hair on the man's wrist at the cuff of his sleeve.

"Our planet can't sustain us any longer," he added, his voice grave. He looked over to his partner, a woman with sharp eyes, and gave her a signal. She clicked a remote in her hand, enhancing our view to include a holographic moon.

"As we continue to veer off course in our orbit around the Sun, so does the moon," he explained, leaving us puzzled. "As we continue to veer off course in our orbit around the Sun, so does the moon in our orbit," He explained.

I didn't understand what he meant but I wasn't the only one, as several of the men in suits voiced their concerns.

"Mr. Dorian, are you saying the moon is getting closer to us?" a man in a suit demanded, his voice calm yet cutting through the room's murmur. The others fell silent and awaited Mr. Dorian's answer.

The astrophysicist nodded, his expression somber. "President Pike, we suspect the moon will collide with Earth within ten years."

The crowd began to murmur again as President Pike of Atlanticanera ran his hand through his hair.

The President cleared his throat and asked, "Did we cause this to happen?" His voice carrying a hint of fear.

Mr. Dorian sighed, his gaze swept across the room, landing on me of all people before turning to his partner. "That's right, I'm afraid. We shifted the planet with our artificial continents," he confessed.

I looked over to see what President Pike's response would be but he seemed to be busy with his paperwork. His family had bought into the Presidential line years ago and become a dynasty since.

"Using data from the past three decades we've concluded that's the cause, and our outcome, " Mr. Dorian said. He turned again to his fellow astrophysicist and signaled for her to change the display.

The image of Earth looked the same at first glance, but the more I looked the differences became clear.

The planet was positioned at another angle and as they zoomed out the sun and moon were further away.

I don't remember what was said over the next few minutes but I remember when everyone noticed the anomaly.

It was hard to miss in the projection of Earth from thirty years prior. It feels weird to see and hear about events from before my birth.

"What is that?" he whispered, more to himself than to the room.

The dated projection of Earth's orbit around the Sun held a dangerous secret.

"Are we all seeing this?" Mr. Dorian asked. His voice sounded both nervous and thrilled.

In the center of the room, in the distant stars around Earth and the Sun, we saw a pair of eyes look back at us.

"Nothing was there before," Ms. Dragoo, his partner, confirmed, her voice tinged with awe and fear.

"You're right, Ms. Dragoo," Mr. Dorian replied. His curiosity was growing with the rest of the room's audible concerns.

They brought up a live feed and turned the satellite's attention over to the coordinates of the eyes. Sure enough, the extraterrestrial stared back at us through the abyss in real-time.

"Something's not right," Ms. Dragoo pointed out. She pointed to the readings coming from the projection.

"Look," Ms. Dragoo added, "our live feed display isn't synched with the old display."

Mr. Dorian analyzed the two data charts and then looked at the hologram projecting the eyes.

"My stars, you're sure it's gotten closer?" Mr. Dorian gasped, his face pale.

I felt a chill and a sinking feeling as I wondered what could be out there among the stars.

"This creature must be astronomical for us to only see its eyes," Mr. Dorian stated, in awe of the discovery.

"Mr. Dorian," President Pike called out, "It would appear that this thing is approaching us, is that right?" The room awaited the astrophysicist's response.

"It would appear so," Mr. Dorian replied. The two astrophysicists continued to study the data for a few more minutes.

President Pike stood from his seat, his posture regal yet shaken and addressed the room. "We came to discuss evacuation," President Pike stated, "And now this. Earth can no longer house twelve billion people, we've ignored the risks for too long. This must be our final sign to do what our ancestors refused to do; leave the Earth behind."

His speech was met with mixed reactions, some hopeful, others despairing. "Even if we wanted to leave, we don't have enough ships," someone protested.

"Where would we even go?" another voice echoed.

President Pike turned to the astrophysicists and asked them something under his breath. The next thing I remember is them discussing an old mech program. It all happened so fast.

They classified the summit's revelations. As far as the public was concerned they would only know of the moon's impending collision in ten years. I was taken with my fellow Sentries to be placed in cryosleep.

It was decided that we would pilot warmechs to confront this 'Astronomical.' I'd never heard the word before today, but that's what they're calling the alien. We were told they would wake us when our mission was ready to begin.

THE *BEGINNING*

I awoke just like I would any other day, only this time I was in a vat of gel connected to medical equipment. *My vision returned after about thirty minutes out of the cryo-tank. The scientist that tended to me said my sense of taste and smell would take longer to return.*

She told me that we were aboard a ship in space on our way toward a space station, Pendulum. I didn't believe her when she said the year was 2420, meaning I had been asleep for nine years. She told me that the evacuation process on Earth had been going well. After she left me alone in my bunk I began to wonder if she even knew the threat that was approaching.

I didn't have an old life, but any remnants of it were surely gone. The only comfort I had was looking out the window at the dark void of space. We would soon be at Pendulum, where my warmech awaited me. All Sentries had firsthand knowledge of how to fly a plane, so I wasn't too worried about the controls.

Upon my arrival at Pendulum, they rushed me into my flight suit, which was the key to plloting the giant mech. In the hangar, I stood in awe of my warmech. It had a sleek design with legs like skyscrapers leading up to its massive body. I couldn't believe something so large could fit inside a space station.

I quickly realized my mech was not the only one in the hangar, as the four others were lined up alongside mine. There was no sign of my fellow Sentries but I found my way to an elevator shaft leading up to the head of mine. Inside the head of the mech was the control room where I'd be piloting the humanlike ship.

As the hangar doors opened, I took control of the machine's steering mechanisms and got a feel for its arms. The whole thing moved flawlessly as I steered it. During my nine-year cryosleep, flight simulation training had been implanted into my memories. I inspected the palms of the warmech and found the barrel of a weapon in each hand. The ship's core was in the chest and it fed energy directly into the palm blasters. My thrusters were operational so I detached my anchors, joining the others in flight.

Our kamikaze mission against the Astronomical had begun.

My whole life I'd been afraid to die, but all I could do now was smile knowing my life had been given purpose.

A few minutes after we had left the docks my comms signal beeped with an incoming message. I reached up to the ear of my spacesuit and joined the open channel.

"This is Jace Garvey, none of us had time for formal introductions," A male voice chimed through my earpiece. On my display I saw Jace using his mech motioning us over.

"Debin Ronn," Another male voice called out. His tone was more upbeat and had more youth to it. He flew up to join Jace at his side.

"I'm Hammers," I stated. My comm was muted so no one heard my first introduction.

"I'm Hammers Nole," I called out again once my mic was on. My fellow Sentries waved to me as the last two joined the chat.

"Kurt Wellis here," Kurt's gravelly voice spoke.

I looked through the display at everyone as we drifted along in the circle our mechs formed in space.

"My name's Twila Marrick," The final Sentry said. Her voice was confident through the mic as she followed up by asking, "Can we get this mission going?"

I swallowed the lump in my throat as we all seemed to share her sentiment.

Jace and Kurt took over the conversation as they discussed our mission. Each of our warmechs was equipped with a nuclear core capable of powering our weaponry. Our mission was to reach the Astronomical and shoot it out of the sky. If that plan failed our second chance at stopping the alien would be self-destruction. Our cores were set to detonate only if all five of us triggered them together.

Once we were all clear on the mission we turned our attention to the threat coming towards Earth.

Jace flew at the front of the pack as we piloted through space. Kurt and Twila were behind me as I raced to catch up to Jace. When I caught up to his identical warmech I saw its head turn to me and nod. I controlled the body of my ship and returned the gesture to him then waved to pass.

We were flying at twenty-five percent thrust as we cruised along.

"Yo, check this out!" Debin Ronn called out. We slowed to look around for the fifth member of our pack but I couldn't see him anywhere.

a second later everyone was in awe as Debin's warmech stood on top of an asteroid as he surfed through space. He used his mech to reach down and grab the rocky object and then his thrusters launched him forward. As Debin's mech gained momentum through space its mechanical hands released the rock. He struggled to pilot the mech as it stood back up on the asteroid.

Debin kept this routine going for several minutes until it lost its appeal.

I kept my focus on the stars ahead of us. Our warmechs traveled at incredible speeds as the sun behind us lingered, watching us. I triggered my autopilot systems to locate Earth but it was no longer visible in the vacuum of space.

"If we continue at this speed our ETA for the Astronomical is eighteen hours," Twila commented. She was alone on the comms for several minutes as I assumed I wasn't the only person on mute.

"Okay, let's sync up and activate autopilot," Jace finally replied. The five of us gathered to fly in formation.

"We'll take shifts as lead pilot so everyone can be mentally prepared for the assault," Jace added.

I unmuted myself to volunteer to pilot us all first but Kurt beat me to it. I managed to take the second *shift and used my time to catch up on human history over the last nine years.*

President Pike passed away five years ago and his son took over. Not much had changed regarding policy, but there was a vote to build a planet and colonize a new homeworld. Construction on the manmade world was set to be completed sometime later this year.

None of that matters if we fail, I thought to myself. It was finally my turn to take the lead on our flight. We were less than fifteen hours from our destiny as I increased our group's speed by two percent. I figured nobody else would notice our acceleration and I appeared to be right. I continued along through space steering my team along the way. An hour had passed before I saw anything noteworthy. A large reflective object hurdled through space in the distance. My scanners told me it was a comet made of icy materials. I fought every urge I had to go off course and get a closer look.

I was halfway through my shift when I increased our speed by another three percent. We were still only using thirty percent of our power but still nobody seemed to notice the change.

The next thing I knew my comms were going off again with an incoming message.

Ah c'mon, I thought to myself. I accepted the chat and unmuted myself.

"Yes?" I spoke into my mic. I expected to hear Jace or Kurt on the other end but instead, I only heard breathing.

"Hello?" I asked, trying to figure out if the connection was going through. I checked the monitor for the ID of the pilot on the other end but it was blank.

"Who is this?" I asked again. The breathing continued for a few more seconds before I'd had enough.

"Okay, well I'm not hearing anything so I'm going to disconnect," I warned. I reached out to end the chat but the breathing on the other end stopped.

I tried to listen for more but all I could hear were faint voices that sounded distant in the background so I hung up.

A second later my comms signalled again for another incoming chat.

"What?" I fired off into my mic, expecting to hear nothing on the other end. Instead, I was greeted by a man's voice I couldn't quite recognize.

"Who am I speaking with?" The man asked. He had a welcoming tone of voice in my earpiece. I looked around wondering where the connection could be coming from. We were alone in the middle of space heading toward the Astronomical. Oh my god, I thought, Is this the alien?

"Are you an alien?" I asked with excitement and concern. The man on the other end sighed before he responded.

"Do I sound like an alien?" he questioned back, then added, "Tell me your name, and I'll tell you mine."

I had heard his voice somewhere once before, but I couldn't quite place where.

"My name is Hammers Nole," I said, "Now, what's your name?"

The voice on the other end laughed to himself.

Does he know who I am? I wondered as he cleared his throat.

"Out here in the riches of space, I'm known as SixBeards," The man proclaimed. "You probably haven't had a chance to hear about me yet," He bragged, "But I'm a famous space pirate." His voice was confident but my recollection of world history was still fresh in my head.

"Funny, I have studied up on the new worlds, both natural and manmade. I don't remember your name in the news," I remarked.

SixBeards scoffed loudly in my ear.

"You're a Sentry, you've only known propaganda your whole life," SixBeards argued. A chill ran down my spine as he shouted in my ear.

"President Pike kept secrets from the world and you and I know it, you don't think you've been lied to in other ways?" SixBeards yelled.

I thought about what he was saying to me as I alerted my teammates.

"Where are you now?" I asked, "You must be close to signal me."

Jace, Kurt, and Twila joined my second chat, where I was relaying SixBeards to them. Where's Debin? I thought to myself. I checked his mech readings and everything was normal.

"I followed you from Pendulum," SixBeards declared.

I checked to make sure Jace and the others could hear, then asked, "Why are you following us?" Before he could answer Debin Ronn joined in to listen. Well, that's a relief, I thought. I muted SixBeards and switched to chat with the others.

"Are you guys hearing this?" I asked. I made sure everyone responded so I wouldn't miss their voices.

"Debin, what took you so long?" Jace asked what we were all thinking.

Debin laughed and then responded, "Am I the only one that's had to use the bathroom in these ridiculous suits? I wanted a little privacy.""

Fair enough, I thought, as I returned to SixBeards' chat. He was midsentence but I didn't miss what he was saying while I was in the other group.

"I want to see her again," SixBeards answered while I was busy chatting with the others.

"I want to see Atrosita once more before she kills us all," Sixbeards shouted as I joined back into his chat.

"Atrosita? Is that the alien's name?" I asked. I'd never heard such a name, and saying it gave me a weird sensation.

SixBeards laughed, then said, "She's more than an alien. She is an Astronomical, sent to us from the heavens."

I laughed but that offended the space pirate on the other end of the call.

"You'll see her for what she truly is soon," SixBeards snarled. He ended the chat abruptly.

Well, that was something else, I thought.

"Did everyone hear that?" I asked as I joined back into the other chat.

The five of us determined that we wouldn't let SixBeards distract us as we continued on our mission. I finished my shift and Debin and Jace took the third watch together in case SixBeards reemerged.

THE MIDDLE

I must have nodded off because when I woke up everyone was arguing with each other in my earpiece. The first thing I noticed was that our warmechs' speeds had increased to forty percent.

"Debin, keep focusing your firepower on the hull of the ship," Jace ordered. Debin Ronn's mech flew backward beside me as it fired energy projectiles from its palms. Each burst of energy created a ripple of static feedback in our comms.

I steered my mech around to face the same direction as Debin's. A massive spacecraft followed close behind us. The hull of the ship had a diamond shape to it with large wings stretched out horizontally. The wingspan of the ship was three times longer than the ship's body, and equal in size to our mechs dimensions.

"Is it SixBeards?" I called out, joining Debin Ronn in his defenses actions.

"Yep," Jace shouted back through the static in our comms.

I steered the long arms of my warmech and joined them together at the palms where I began to charge my ship's energy. The mechanical fingers of my mech contained an orb of energy charging up in my hands as I extended my arms forward. The resulting release radiated from my mech's palms like sunlight. The projectile blast burned through the wing of SixBeards' ship, severing it. My squad and I cheered as the wing's engine erupted into flames.

"Why did he attack us?" I asked as we put distance between us and the pirate's ship.

The static in our comms had faded after the last attack.

"We're close to Atrosita," Jace replied. I began to wonder how long I had been asleep and before I could ask I saw a wall of white up ahead.

"What is that wall up there?" I asked the group. We accelerated towards it as Twila remarked, "That's Atrosita." I couldn't believe how big she was. I felt chills run up and down my spine along with a shiver as I tried to shake the feeling.

How could something be so big, I wondered to myself, she's all I see.

"Are we going to attack soon?" I blurted into the comms. The group didn't immediately respond, so I asked a second time.

Space shifted ahead of me as I watched the wall of white slowly close.

"What was that?" I asked, "Where did she go?" I scanned my monitors but they weren't picking up anything.

"Hammers," Jace said softly, "That was Atrosita's eye. She just blinked."

No way! I thought to myself. I scanned my monitors again but Atrosita's body must have been too large to identify.

"What do we do?" I asked. I didn't expect an answer, I was in shock.

"We call the astrophysicist, Mr. Dorian," Jace replied, "I think his calculations may have been off."

A minute later we were sending a long-distance satellite call back to Earth.

The call rang three times before a woman answered.

"Howdy," She said.

"Hello," Jace replied, "You're not going to believe this, but my name is Jace Garvey. I'm one of the Sentries in space right now, is Mr. Dorian there?"

The woman on the other end mumbled something then said, "Yes, he's here, not that it'll do you much good."

Jace sighed then asked, "Why is that, ma'am?"

The woman on the other end became emotional and glanced away, "Because," She said, "He's lost his damn mind." She broke down crying, "You guys must be figuring it out by now, huh? Well he did, what a fool, He got his calculations wrong, drove him mad."

Jace gave his apologies and then ended the connection.

"Now what?" Debin Ronn asked.

The five of us drifted through space as we all contemplated our plan of action.

"Can't we just attack like we'd planned?" I finally asked, "I thought we had all come to die, so what did it matter if Atrosita was larger than anticipated?"

I looked out to see the Astronomical's large sclera filling my view.

"I don't think a standard attack would have any effect," Jace sighed, "So that only leaves one other option. We fly straight into her and self-destruct, and pray we take her with us."

I was ready, but Kurt and Twila had another idea.

"Or," Kurt said, "We take these warmechs and we get the hell out of here." Twila chimed in to agree with Kurt.

"Exactly," Twila added, "They sent out here to die, but we can start over, I say we take our chances."

Debin Ronn had been quiet the whole time but I was curious to know what his thoughts.

"What do you think, Debin?" I asked over the comms. He didn't immediately respond, which worried me. I looked over to his mech with my monitors and awaited his opinion.

"Jace, there's no self-destruction sequence if we don't all initiate it," Debin commented. I wasn't sure where he was going with his remark.

"Kurt, Twila," Debin added, "We have the opportunity to save mankind, they'll write songs about us. We've gotta do this."

The five of us took a moment of silence before Kurt responded.

"You're on your own," Kurt replied. He did not hesitate to break free from the group and fly away. Twila followed close behind as we all chased after them.

"Get back here!" Jace cried out over the comms. Kurt and Twila cut their comms on us as they increased their thrusters to escape.

Jace extended his palm out toward Kurt and Twila ahead of us and began to fire at them. Jace's blast connected with Twila's leg thrusters causing her to spin out of control. As that happened Debin Ronn's warmech caught up to Kurt's and tackled him off-course.

The two machines grappled through space as Kurt fought to aim at Debin's mech. Debin did everything he could to avoid Kurt's attack as his assailant rejoined our group chat.

"If you want to die so badly then allow me to help you!" Kurt yelled into our headsets. His warmech climbed onto Debin's and he wrapped his hands around Debin's mech's head. As his attack charged up Debin pleaded through the comms channel for Kurt to stop.

I charged toward Kurt and Debin and launched round after round of my own at Kurt's mech. My barrage of energy blasts threw Kurt's mech back, preventing his kill shot on Debin. As Kurt's mech spiraled out of control he carried Debin's mech with him.

Kurt used his thrusters to increase the pair's momentum as they flew away from us.

"Kurt stop!" Debin cried out across the comms channel again. He tried to stabilize them with his own mech's thrusters but it backfired, adding to their speed. I looked over to Jace's mech and saw he was busy subduing Twila.

I launched forward again on my way to Kurt and Debin as I realized they were traveling toward Atrosita's eye.

"Kurt!" I shouted at the two ahead of me. I reached out my mech's right arm for another shot at Kurt's thrusters and fired, hoping to slow them down. My attack landed in an explosion of sparks and light against the head of Kurt's mech, killing him in an instant.

"I didn't mean to do that," I cried out over the comms, "I was aiming for Kurt's thrusters." It didn't matter what I said. I watched Kurt's smoking mech pull Debin's ship into Atrosita's eye because I overshot my mark.

"Debin! I'm sorry!" I yelled into my mic as I saw their mechs explode on impact with the Astronomical's eye, stunning the space kaiju.

"Guys," I cried, "I'm sorry." I muted myself to scream. We needed all five of us to activate the self-destruct sequence, and that was our last line of defense. I screamed until my throat hurt, ignoring Jace and Twila on the comms. I ripped my earpiece out so I could be alone as I stared at the display in front of me. Atrosita's eye was still closed from the explosion earlier.

Everything about this is wrong, I thought to myself. Our calculations about the Astronomical were wrong from the start. I thought back to what felt like yesterday, in that summit chamber.

SixBeards said President Pike was lying to us about something. I grabbed my earpiece and reinserted it into my ear. Jace and Twila were waiting for me on the comms when I returned to the channel.

"I'm going to call SixBeards," I said. There was a pause after I spoke which I used to dial in SixBeards. The space pirate didn't answer the first invite so I sent a second one.

"Ah, what the hell do you want?" SixBeards fired off as he joined the call. I cleared my throat and then replied.

"We need your help," I said as I watched for Atrosita beyond my mech. Jace and Twila were focused on the Astronomical as well.

"You said President Pike was lying to us," I spoke again, "What was he lying about?" Outside my mech, I could see Atrosita's eyelid opening slowly.

SixBeards exhaled deeply in my ear. "Well for starters, they discovered Atrosita forty years ago," The space pirate said.

"We had plenty of time to evacuate the Earth, but Pike waited until it was too late," SixBeards continued. Atrosita's eye was fully opened now, but she blinked as if she were still stunned.

"Why would he do that?" Jace asked, joining the conversation.

"For control," SixBeards said, "Pike made sure he had control over everything. Now his son is the president of three planets, well, until Atrosita reaches Earth."

I checked my monitors again to survey Atrosita, but she hadn't had any change.

"Why is she coming to Earth?" Jace asked. SixBeards didn't have an answer as he sighed.

"Guys," Twila interrupted, "Look." I turned my attention to the monitors, where I saw the blood-orange iris of her eye staring back at us. I pilot my warmech up to get a better view of her pupil, where we make eye contact through the display.

"Don't look into her eyes," SixBeards shouted into the comms. I shut my eyes quickly before anything could happen but Jace and Twila were affected by Atrosita.

They turned their warmechs on mine while my eyes were closed and began to pull my mech apart.

"Stop!" I cried out as my systems began to fade.

"Hammers, you're gonna have to emergency eject!" SixBeards shouted through my faint comms. I looked for the trigger as my monitors continued to flicker in and out.

I found the emergency switch and flipped it repeatedly hoping my mech had enough power. As the head of my mech detached from the neck and torso, the force from the ejection pulled me into my seat. I couldn't breathe as the head accelerated away from the body of my mech.

As I flew away helpless in my craft I saw Atrosita approaching my former mech. Her Astronomical mouth engulfed my view with rows and rows of planet-shattering teeth. I narrowly escaped as her jaws clenched just beyond my escape pod, devouring my two former allies.

"Hold on bud," SixBeards called out. I couldn't believe that we were still in contact after my evacuation but I was relieved to hear his voice. As I hurdled through space SixBeards' damaged ship managed to catch up to me, risking his life in the process. SixBeards ship launched a harpoon into my mech's escape pod, reeling me into safety.

I exited my craft and ran off the landing dock and down a long corridor to the captain's deck. SixBeards was the lone survivor in his massive ship, focused in his captain's chair. When I reached him I knew I had recognized his voice from somewhere.

"Adrian?" I called out in shock. He had aged since the day I met him at the summit.

"Hello Hammers," Adrian replied. He smiled briefly after saying my name.

"But why are you doing all of this?" I asked. I glanced around at his former crew dead at their workstations and along the floors.

He kept his eyes focused on our ship's trajectory.

"We left the Sentries together. I led this crew to Atrosita, but her eyes possessed us," Adrian said, "We fought for her love. I was under her control ever since, until those other pilots broke her gaze just now."

The space kaiju on our tails kept up behind us as she chased our damaged ship through space. I looked around and found an empty copilot seat near Adrian. I strapped myself in as a computer interface lit up before my eyes. The ship's remaining engines were being overworked to make up for the damage I'd caused to the other wing. We had enough energy output to take us back to Earth, but we knew Atrosita was heading there with or without us.

"Adrian," I said, "I have an idea. It's too late for us to save Earth, but we can give the people more time." I showed him the coordinates I'd mapped out for us.

"That's suicidal," Adrian called out over his shoulder. He kept his focus on navigating us toward Earth.

"We can't fly to the sun Hammers," Adrian continued to shout, "We'd be fried before we got there."

I got up from my seat and placed a hand on Adrian's shoulder, and said, "I'm sorry you got involved. My mission was to die today along with Atrosita, that's the way I want it to be."

Adrian pulled his shoulder away from my hand.

"Why are you choosing death to save people who didn't want us to exist in the first place?" He questioned.

I thought about it for a moment and gave him a shrug. "I guess, because even though I don't care about the rest of humanity," I said, "I think they still deserve a chance to live."

Adrian thought about my words and then told me to return to my seat.

"You're sure this plan will work?" He asked. I smiled and replied, "If we can get her to follow us then I'm sure we can kill Atrosita with the Sun." Adrian maneuvered our ship around and opened fire on Atrosita as we rocketed forward on a new path. Up ahead of us, a bright yellow star lit the darkness of space. The closer we got the more I felt its warmth and energy. I once heard that the Sun could be felt like this from Earth, and as we approach I hope for humanity to feel its touch again. Our ship began to signal us of extreme heat conditions as the star filled our view with light.

"This is it," Adrian declared.

"This is it," I repeat Adrian's words as I'm blinded.

As I felt myself go I began to feel an unexplainable connection with Atrosita. She reveals to me that we were wrong about her this entire time. She was never interested in Earth, we meant nothing to her, just as I meant nothing to the EU. This Astronomical alien came for our Sun, as she has for countless other stars. What she'll leave behind is nothing, but then I remember, Nothing kills the Sun.

THE END

www.ingramcontent.com/pod-product-compliance
Lightning Source LLC
Chambersburg PA
CBHW021324160726
47994CB00004B/1594